THE ADVENTURES OF
TOM SAWYER

MARK TWAIN

ADAPTED BY VALERIE TRIPP

ILLUSTRATED BY ROSALIA RADOSTI

CHAPTER 1

"TOM!"

Tom Sawyer heard his Aunt Polly call him. But he was happily hidden in a corner of the kitchen, sneaking spoonfuls of jam out of the jar, so he didn't answer.

"Tom!" Aunt Polly called again.

And again, Tom kept still. He did not like being scolded—but he did like jam!

"Where is that boy?" Aunt Polly fussed. She searched all around, even poking the broom under the furniture, and . . .

Meow!

Aunt Polly surprised the cat under the couch! The cat sprang up yowling and then sped away as fast as it could.

Aunt Polly opened the door and looked for Tom in the garden. But he wasn't hiding behind the tangled tomato vines or among the deep-green weeds. Aunt Polly shaded her eyes. The bright sun shone down hot on the

little town of St. Petersburg, Missouri, which nestled next to the wide Mississippi River.

"Yoo-hoo, Tom!" Aunt Polly shouted.

Tom decided this was a good time to make his get-away. But Aunt Polly was too quick for him. Just as he tried to slip behind her and out the door, Aunt Polly turned, and *swoosh*! She caught him.

"There you are! Look at your hands! Look at your mouth! I've told and told you to leave that jam alone," Aunt Polly sighed. "What ever shall I do with you, Tom?"

But before Aunt Polly could answer her own question, Tom said, "My! Look behind you, Aunt!"

Aunt Polly whirled around to see what Tom was talking about, and *zoom*! Tom fled, lickety-split, across the room and out the door. As fast as he could, Tom ran through the yard. He leapt up, grabbed the top of the fence, and vaulted over, landing on the other side with a *thud*. Then he sped away, quick as a flash.

Aunt Polly stood surprised for a moment. She sounded exasperated with Tom—and herself—when she said, "That scamp has fooled me again." She sighed and shook her head. "He's such a trickster. Well, I'll have to give him chores tomorrow to make up for his mischief today. It'll be misery for Tom, watching the other children skylarking and having their Saturday fun, but he has to learn to mend his wild ways. Now, let me think: What boring chore shall I make him do? Wash the windows? Mop the floor? Weed the garden?"

Suddenly, Aunt Polly smiled. She had thought of a dandy chore for Tom to do!

CHAPTER 2

"OH NO." Tom heaved a sigh so deep that it sank from the top of his head all the way down to below his bare toes.

Sure enough, Aunt Polly had thought up a mighty chore for him to do: Tom had to whitewash the fence.

And there were miles and miles of fence! Well, nearly thirty yards' worth, anyway, and the fence was twice as tall as Tom. *This is going to take forever and a day*, he thought miserably.

Tom had a long-handled brush in one hand and a bucket of whitewash in the other. The heavy tools dragged his arms—and his spirits—down into doom and gloom.

It was a bright, fresh Saturday morning, and Tom thought longingly of all the fun he had planned for the day: swimming, fishing, climbing trees, exploring the caves along the riverbank.

It was bitterly unfair that he had to work while his

friends were off on adventures, because he always had the best ideas out of anyone for games to play!

No one would say that Tom was the most well-behaved boy in the village, but they'd probably agree that he was the cleverest one, the one with the wildest imagination, and certainly the one with the greatest ability to stir up excitement and trouble!

Tom's heart was heavy as he surveyed the seemingly endless fence. Then, at this dark and hopeless moment, inspiration burst upon him, and it was nothing less than a great, magnificent idea.

Tom took up his brush and went peacefully to work.

Pretty soon, Tom's friend Ben Rogers came hop-skip-jumping by, tossing a delicious-looking apple from hand to hand. "Hiya! You're up a stump!" teased Ben.

Tom ignored Ben. Very slowly and carefully, he painted a slat of the fence, looked at it with the eye of an artist, and then gave it another gentle sweep of the brush.

Ben boasted, "I'm going swimming."

Tom turned. "Oh, hello, Ben," he said. "I didn't notice you."

"I said, I'm going swimming, and you have to work!" said Ben.

"What do you call work?" asked Tom, tilting his head and looking at Ben.

"Why, isn't that work?" asked Ben. "Whitewashing a fence?"

Tom went back to painting and answered carelessly, "Well, maybe it is, and maybe it isn't. All I know is, it suits Tom Sawyer."

"Oh, come now," said Ben. "You don't mean to let on that you like it?"

"Like it?" said Tom, smoothing a broad brushstroke across the fence. "Well, I don't see why I shouldn't like it. Does a boy get a chance to whitewash a fence every day?"

Ben stopped tossing his apple. It had never occurred to him that whitewashing was anything anyone would ever want to do. As he watched Tom sweep his brush back and forth, adding a touch here and there to make the paint perfect, Ben became more and more absorbed, and more and more interested, and more and more envious of Tom.

"Say, Tom, let me whitewash awhile," Ben said.

Tom considered, but then said, "No, no, you better not. Aunt Polly is awfully particular about this fence. It's got to be done just so. I reckon there's not one boy in a thousand, maybe two thousand, that can do it the way it's got to be done."

"Oh, come on now, let me just try," wheedled Ben. "I'd let you, Tom, if you were me."

"Ben, I'd like to let you paint," said Tom, "but if anything were to happen to this fence—"

"I'll be careful!" insisted Ben. "Let me try. I'll give you the core of my apple."

"Well, here," Tom said. He started to give Ben the paintbrush and then took it back. "No, Ben, no. I'm afraid—"

"I'll give you *all* of my apple!" said Ben.

Tom gave Ben the brush. He pretended to be reluctant, but secretly he was happy: he had fooled Ben into begging to paint the fence for him!

While Ben worked and sweated, Tom sat in the shade nearby, munched his apple, and waited. When Ben was tired, Billy Fisher came by and traded Tom a kite for the chance to whitewash, and then when Billy got tired, Johnny Miller came by.

On and on, hour after hour, Tom talked boy after boy into wanting to paint the fence. By the end of the afternoon, Tom had tricked his way to quite a collection of items: the apple and the kite, plus twelve marbles, a key that wouldn't open anything, a dog collar without a dog, four pieces of orange peel, a tin soldier, and some

tadpoles. He'd had a good, lazy time, chatting with his friends and watching them work. The fence had three gleaming, dazzling fresh coats of paint. It would have had more if Tom hadn't run out of whitewash.

Best of all, Tom had made two very important discoveries: First, to make someone want something, make it hard to get. And second, work's what we have to do, and play's what we don't have to do.

Whistling cheerfully, with his treasures in his pockets, Tom went off to find Aunt Polly. "May I go and play now, Aunt?" he asked.

"What? Already?" asked Aunt Polly. "How much painting have you done?"

"It's all done, Aunt," answered Tom.

"Hmph," snorted Aunt Polly. She didn't believe it. She went out to see for herself, and when she found the entire fence not only whitewashed, but also coated and recoated so that it shone blindingly bright, she was astonished. In fact, Aunt Polly was so happy with Tom's work that she brought him to the kitchen and gave him a choice apple, saying, "It would be a very good thing if you'd work that hard all the time, Tom. Go along now and play."

Tom skipped off merrily, and Aunt Polly didn't even notice that he sneaked a doughnut as he went on his way.

CHAPTER 3

PROUD AND PLEASED AFTER his fence-painting triumph, Tom swaggered along the road. As he passed his friend Jeff Thatcher's house, he saw someone he'd never seen before—a girl with yellow braids and big, blue eyes.

Tom began to show off to make the new girl notice him. He did cartwheels and headstands, backflips and somersaults. He walked on his hands. He balanced a straw on his nose. Right in the middle of a dangerous trick, Tom saw the girl was turning away and going inside the house.

But just before she disappeared, the girl tossed a pansy over the fence. Tom pretended he wasn't at all interested in picking up the flower, but later he tucked it into his jacket as close to his heart as he could. Tom had made up his mind: he had a crush on the new girl and hoped they could be friends.

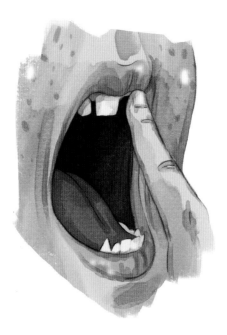

Wiggle! One of Tom's upper front teeth was loose. *Wiggle, wiggle.* He wiggled his loose tooth back and forth.

It was Monday morning, and Tom didn't want to go to school. It wasn't that Tom didn't like school, exactly. He was the best reader in the class. He'd memorized whole sections of *Robin Hood and His Merry Men* and knew books about pirates by heart! He was very good at drawing and geography, and he'd been the proud winner of the spelling award for three months in a row. But Tom would always rather be outside. Time passed so slowly indoors!

Wiggle, wiggle. Maybe he could pretend that his loose

tooth hurt so much that he couldn't go to school. But Aunt Polly would probably pull the tooth out, and that would really hurt. So Tom decided to pretend his toe hurt instead.

Tom moaned so loud and long about his toe that Aunt Polly came to his room and asked, "What ails you, child?"

"Oh, Aunt, my sore toe's mortified," said Tom. He wasn't sure what "mortified" meant, but it sounded dire. "My toe's going to fall off!"

Aunt Polly laughed. "Stop your nonsense!"

Tom, feeling a bit foolish, said, "My toe seems mortified. It hurts so badly that I don't mind my loose tooth that aches perfectly awful."

"Loose tooth, is it?" said Aunt Polly. "I know this fuss is all because you want to skip school and go fishing. Oh, Tom! You'll wear me out with your outrageous-ness." Then, *plink*! Aunt Polly pulled out Tom's loose tooth with a silk thread and sent him off to school.

Losing a tooth's not so bad, thought Tom. He liked spit-ting through the gap in his teeth.

And when he ran into his friend Huckleberry Finn, he made a good bargain, trading his tooth for a beetle. Now late, Tom rushed off to school.

"Thomas Sawyer!" barked the teacher. "Late again! As punishment, go sit with the girls."

"Yes, sir," said Tom.

Giggles, winks, and whispers rippled around the room. Tom blushed—but not because he was ashamed. He was pleased. Rascally Tom wanted the punishment because the only empty seat was next to the new girl, Becky Thatcher, and Tom had a crush on her.

Tom sat next to Becky and put a peach in front of her. She pushed the peach away. Tom gently put it back. Becky pushed it away again. Tom patiently put the peach in front of Becky again. This time, she let it stay.

Tom drew pictures on his slate for Becky—first a house, then a man.

"I wish I could draw," said Becky.

"I'll teach you," said Tom. He gave Becky a piece of gum and asked, "Would you like to promise to be best friends forever?"

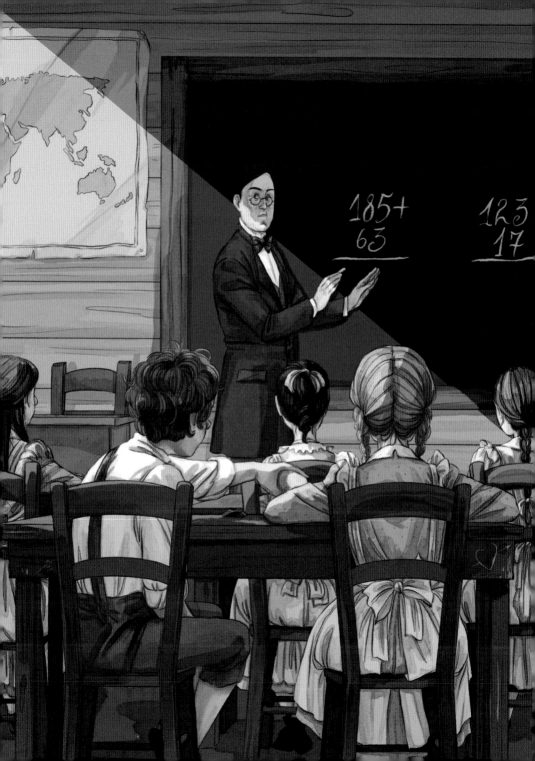

"Well," said Becky, "how do you do that?"

"Oh, it's fun!" said Tom. "When Amy Lawrence and I promised—"

Becky's face fell. "You've done this before?" she said angrily. "So I'd be your second-best best friend?"

"No, I mean, yes, I mean—" Tom struggled to explain.

But it was too late. Becky refused to listen.

Later, when they were outside, Tom tried desperately to impress her. He yelled and laughed and whooped. He chased the other boys and jumped over the fence. He even did a few handsprings and stood on his head. But when he fell, sprawling right under Becky's nose, she just turned up that very nose and said, "Mfff! Some people think they're mighty smart—always showing off!"

Tom's cheeks burned. He gathered himself up and sneaked off, devastated. Tom's heart was broken, but his mind was made up: he'd run away. Then Becky would miss him and be sorry she'd treated him coldly!

CHAPTER 4

AS TOM STARTED DOWN THE ROAD, he came upon his friend Joe Harper looking as sad and mad as Tom felt. "What's the matter?" Tom asked.

"My mother scolded me for drinking some sweet cream that I never touched!" protested Joe. "I'm going to be a hermit and live in a cave. That'll make Mother sorry."

"I'm running away too," said Tom, "to be a pirate. Call me the Captain Avenger of the Spanish Main. I'll sail the seven seas, looking for treasure. Being a pirate's more fun than being a hermit. Come with me!"

"I will!" said Joe happily. "Call me the Terror of the Seas."

Tom and Joe invited Huckleberry Finn to join them. "You'll be Huck the Red-Handed," said Tom.

"Suits me," said Huck.

"Now, my hearties! Steady as she goes!" ordered Tom.

"Aye, aye, sir!" answered Joe and Huck.

The three bold boys met at a lonely spot on the riverbank at midnight, found a raft, and shoved off to float down the river to Jackson Island. They pretended the raft was a sailing ship tossed on the wickedly raging seas, even though, really, the river was calm.

They soon landed safely on Jackson Island. No one lived there. It was unexplored and wild.

"This is the life!" Tom sighed happily as the boys feasted on cornmeal biscuits and bacon that Joe had brought from home. "We don't have to get up in the morning. We don't have to go to school and wash—all that's foolishness. Pirates have a fine old time. They find money and bury it, and they wear clothes made of gold and silver."

After their snack, the boys used an old sail to make a raggedy tent to store their gear.

"Let's sleep out under the stars, like real pirates do," said Tom the Captain Avenger. Joe the Terror of the Seas and Huck the Red-Handed agreed. Huck fell right asleep, but Tom and Joe had a harder time.

"Tom, do you think maybe it was wrong to run away?" whispered Joe. "Should we go back?"

"I dunno," said Tom. His conscience bothered him too. He was sorry for making Aunt Polly worry and even sorrier he'd taken a ham from her kitchen. "Seems like it was wrong to steal the food."

"Let's promise never to steal again," said Joe.

"I promise," said Tom, even though that made him an unusual pirate, since pirate treasure was often stolen.

When Tom awoke in the cool, gray dawn, he was

glad he had stayed. He didn't miss the village at all. The island was full of life: Ladybugs and butterflies flitted in the sunshine. Worms, ants, and turtles crawled past. A fox and a squirrel scurried by. Woodpeckers hammered, and birds sang. All nature was awake and stirring on this wonderful morning.

The other boys soon woke up. Huck made drinking cups out of hickory leaves, and the thirsty boys drank fresh, cool water from a spring after eating their fill of fish for breakfast.

They explored the island from end to end, running free and happy, shouting and whooping as they chased and tumbled after one another. When they were hot, they jumped in the river, swimming, splashing, sputtering, ducking, dunking, and diving while they laughed and gasped for air. When they were tired of swimming, they played marbles, or rested until they were dry and warm—then did the whole thing all over again until they were completely exhausted.

Once or twice, Joe began to show signs of homesickness, but Tom distracted him by saying, "I bet there've been pirates on this island before, boys, and they've hidden treasure here—chests full of gold and silver. Let's hunt for buried treasure!"

For three days, the trio of boys had a glorious time. But on the third night, a terrible thunderstorm blew in. It began with a moaning wind, then a sweep of chilly air, and then the fierce glare of lightning lit up the forest, followed by deafening peals of thunder that shook the boys to their bones. They clung together in terror, huddling in their raggedy tent until a furious blast of wind tore the sail loose and swept it away. Cold and scared, they took shelter under a great oak tree while, all around them, other giant trees waved their branches crazily, and earsplitting thunder exploded.

When the storm was finally over, the boys went back to where they'd pitched their tent. "Everything is drenched," moaned Joe. "There's not a dry spot to sleep anywhere."

"We'll just have to stay up all night then," said Tom. So the boys did, talking about the awful storm.

When the sun rose the next morning, Joe said, "Let's give it up. I want to go home."

"I reckon I do too," said Huck.

Tom's conscience had made him miserable for making kind old Aunt Polly miserable—so much so that, one night,

he'd momentarily sneaked back home and overheard Aunt Polly talking to Joe's mother about how they missed the boys and how they must make plans for a funeral.

So now Tom said to Joe and Huck, "I s'pose that even the most fun in the world gets dull when there's no one around to impress—or bother! When there's no one to tell me I can't swim or fish or run wild, I hardly want to!"

So Tom the Captain Avenger, Joe the Terror of the Seas, and Huck the Red-Handed agreed to leave the island. They were pretty cheerful about it because they had an outstanding new plan.

The boys chose Sunday to return home because they knew that the whole town, including Tom's aunt and Joe's mother, would be at church. In fact, everyone had gathered at a service to honor Tom, Joe, and Huck. People spoke about how sweet, generous, and noble the boys were, and soon almost everyone was crying.

The back door of the church creaked, and everyone stared as the three dead boys came marching up the aisle: Tom in the lead, Joe next, and Huck in the rear. They had been hidden, listening to their own funeral sermon!

"Tom!" cried Aunt Polly. "Mercy on us! Tom! It's you."

Their friends and family smothered the boys with kisses. Everyone was so relieved that they were back safe and sound.

"Couldn't you have thought to pity us and save us from worry and sorrow?" said Aunt Polly with her eyes full of tears.

"I'm sorry, Aunt Polly," said Tom. "I know now it was mean, letting you think we were drowned. I didn't mean to be mean. I didn't, honest."

After his apology, Tom got more kisses that day than he had earned before in a year, and Betsy promised she'd be his best friend forever.

All in all, Tom thought—while Joe and Huck agreed—they had a very satisfactory homecoming!

CHAPTER 5

WE CAN STILL DIG for buried treasure," said Tom to Huck, "even if we aren't on a deserted island anymore."

"Where'll we dig?" Huck asked.

"Well, we've tried Jackson Island a little," answered Tom. "Let's try that empty old house down in the valley."

Eagerly, the two boys set off with their shovels. But when they reached the lonely old house, they were afraid to go in. The house looked so miserable, baking under the hot sun. The boys crept to the door, entered softly, and spoke in whispers. The house was even more miserable inside than out! It was full of cobwebs. The windows were broken and empty, and there were weeds growing through the floor. The boys climbed up the rickety, twisted staircase and had just begun to explore the upstairs when—

"Shh!" said Tom. "Someone's coming."

The boys lay down and looked through a knothole in the floor. They stopped breathing when they saw two men—robbers!—in the room below.

"What'll we do with this money?" asked one robber.

"Bury it in my den," said the other, "under the 'X.'"

Then the two robbers slipped out of the house and moved swiftly toward the river. Tom and Huck waited until the two men were far away, and then they hurried home, glad to make their escape.

"Let's find that den, Tom," said Huck.

"You bet!" said Tom. "We'll never give up!"

But before Tom and Huck could search for the robbers' den, Tom went on a school picnic with his classmates, organized by his new best friend Becky.

An old ferryboat carried the children to a wooded hollow about three miles down the river from the town. They waded ashore, and soon the forest and hills were echoing with shouts and laughter. After climbing and running, scrambling over rocks, and getting hot and tired, the picnickers ate their feast under the oak trees.

"Who's ready for the cave?" someone asked after lunch. Everybody was, so there they went.

Tom knew the cave very well. Narrow, crooked tunnels led down deep into the earth, turning and twisting like a dark, chilly maze with as many tangled paths to follow as strands in a spiderweb.

"Let's go this way," said Tom to Becky, holding up his candle to light the path. They came to a lacy waterfall. Tom squeezed behind the falling water to illuminate the dark space behind it. "The water's carved a sort of stairway back here. Come and see."

Becky was glad to explore. On and on, she and Tom

wound this way and that on twisted paths that led far down into the secret depths of the cave.

"Oh, Tom, look!" said Becky. She held up her candle, and they both gasped. They were in a spacious cavern full of fantastic pillars made from shining stalactites that hung so far down from the ceiling that they'd joined with stalagmites rising up from the cave floor. In the cavern, there was a beautiful spring surrounded by glittering crystals.

The roof of the cavern was so high that thousands of bats had packed themselves together in tight bunches. Tom and Becky lifted their candles to see the bats.

"Look out!" Tom cried. The candlelight disturbed the bats, and they came flocking down by the hundreds, squeaking and darting furiously at the candles. One bat swooped in so close that—*swoosh!*—it struck Becky's light out with its wings as she was running out of the cavern.

The angry bats chased Tom and Becky, who plunged into every new passage they saw, until at last, free of the bats, they stopped at the edge of a long, dark lake.

"Can you find the way back?" asked Becky. "It's all a mixed-up crookedness to me."

"I reckon I can find the way," said Tom.

They started through a narrow hallway, peering down every dark passage to see if it led to the path out. Again and again, Tom said, "Well, this isn't the one, but we'll come to it right away!" Soon, Tom was so desperate that he led Becky down any path, hoping it would be the right way out. But it never was.

"I'm sure everyone's hunting for us," said Becky.

"I hope they are," said Tom. He shouted until he was hoarse, but no one heard him. "We're way down below everyone, and I don't know how far away north or south or east or whichever it is. We can't hear them, and they can't hear us."

They kept moving because it was dreadful to sit still; moving in some direction, or any direction, was at least progress. But after what felt like hours and hours of aimless wandering, they were too tired to go another step.

At one point, they were able to hear rescuers shouting. Tom and Becky whooped and yelled as long and loud as they could, but in a moment or two, the sounds of the rescuers disappeared.

Hungry, hopeless, and exhausted, Tom and Becky watched their last candle flame flicker out. Then they fell asleep in the dark, dark cave. The weary time dragged on. They slept and slept again, then woke up cold and hungry, sure that the search for them had been given up.

But Tom refused to lose hope. He found a kite string in his pocket and said, "You stay here, Becky, at one end of the string. I'll unwind it as I go along and then follow it back to you so that we won't be separated."

Tom tied one end of the string to a rock and, unwinding the string as he went along, groped his way in the dark. He stretched the kite string as far as it would go down one passage, then another, then another. He was just about to turn back when he glimpsed a far-off speck of . . . light!

Tom scrabbled toward the light, pushed his head and shoulders through a small hole, and saw the broad Mississippi River!

"Becky!" he shouted. "We're saved!"

CHAPTER 6

EVERYONE IN TOWN was so happy to see Tom and Becky that a parade formed as friends pulled them in an open carriage that swept magnificently up the main street. All the bells in the village rang out, and soon the streets were crowded with people banging tin pans, blowing horns, and cheering, "They're found!" After three days and three nights lost in the cave, Tom and Becky were home.

It was the greatest day the little village had ever seen, and Tom and Becky were the heroes of it all.

For any other kid, that would have been enough adventure to last awhile. But not for Tom Sawyer. As soon as he could, Tom set out to find Huck Finn.

"I guess that stolen money's a goner for us, Tom," Huck said sadly.

"Huck, that money is in the cave!" said Tom.

Huck's eyes blazed. "In the cave?"

Tom nodded. "Will you help me get it?"

"You bet I will!" said Huck. "Let's go right now."

Tom tucked kite strings in his pocket. The boys borrowed a boat and set forth at once. When they landed, Huck searched all around for an opening to the cave, but Tom proudly marched straight to a clump of sumac bushes, pulled them aside, and showed Huck the hidden entrance to the cave, saying, "Here it is! The snuggest hole in the country."

The boys wriggled their way through the hole and into the cave. They crawled to the end of the tunnel, tied the kite strings to a rock, and continued. When they passed the dark, sad spot where Tom and Becky had watched their last candle go out, Tom shuddered. The stillness and gloom of the place made the boys eager to move on.

Soon, Tom said, "Now I'll show you something, Huck." Tom held his candle up. "Look around the corner as far as you can. What do you see on that big rock yonder?"

"Tom, it's an 'X'!" said Huck. "The robbers said they'd hide the money under an 'X.'"

"I bet you the money is under that rock!" said Tom.

They dug in the clay, and Tom crawled into a passage under the rock with Huck right behind him. He went first to the right, then to the left, and then exclaimed, "Whoa, Huck, look here!"

It was the treasure box, sure enough, tucked in a snug little corner.

Huck ran his hands through the coins. "Got it, at last," he said. "My, we're rich, Tom!"

In fact, when all the money was counted, Huck and Tom were *very* rich. There was more money in the treasure box than anyone in the town had ever seen before at one time.

Tom and Huck's windfall was talked about, gloated over, and glorified. Wherever the duo went, they were admired as the town's most remarkable boys.

Aunt Polly was especially proud of Tom. "He isn't bad, only mischievous," she said. "In fact, I might even say that Tom's the best-hearted boy that ever was."